For
Debbie Moody

First published 1994 by Walker Books Ltd
87 Vauxhall Walk, London SE11 5HJ

This edition published 2000

2 4 6 8 10 9 7 5 3 1

© 1994 Nick Sharratt

This book has been typeset in AT Arta.

Printed in Singapore

British Library Cataloguing in Publication Data
A catalogue record for this book is
available from the British Library.

ISBN 0-7445-7271-1

Mrs Pirate

Nick Sharratt

WALKER BOOKS

AND SUBSIDIARIES

LONDON • BOSTON • SYDNEY

When Mrs Pirate
went shopping,
she bought
an apple pie

and a patch
for her eye,

a bar
of soap

and a
telescope,

an onion
and a carrot

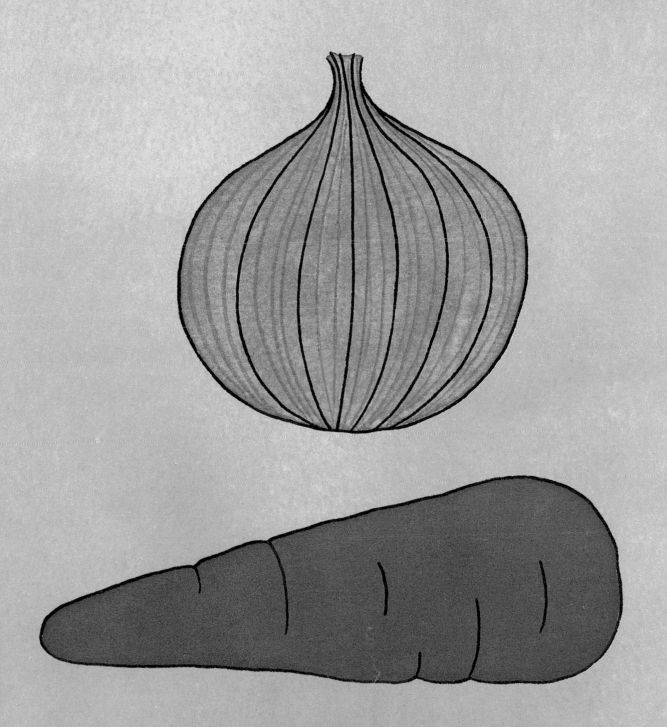

and a red and
green parrot,

some knickers
and a vest

and an old
treasure chest,

buttons for
her coat

and a big
sailing boat,

a packet
of tea

and some sea.